# DISC
# THE AS1

# A JOURNEY
# BEYOND THE
# PHYSICAL

## SWAMINATHAN MURALI

# TABLE OF CONTENTS

|  | | |
|---|---|---|
|  | Prologue | 09 |
| 1 | Interconnected Astral Realms | 15 |
| 2 | Astral Projection as A Common Skill | 24 |
| 3 | The Odyssey of Alex: A Philosophical Journey Beyond the Astral | 32 |
| 4 | Astral Detectives: The Unseen Threads of Reality | 39 |
| 5 | Alex's Odyssey: The Astral Mirror of The Soul | 46 |
| 6 | Alex & the Labyrinth of Time: An Astral Odyssey | 53 |
| 7 | Alex & the Shadows of The Astral: A Cosmic Balance in Peril | 60 |
| 8 | Alex & the Guardians of The Astral: A Quest for Cosmic Conservation | 67 |
| 9 | Alex & the Tapestry of Time: Unraveling The Astral Threads of Cultures | 75 |
| 10 | Alex & the Echoes of The Astral War | 83 |
| 11 | Alex & the Quest for The Astral Artifacts | 91 |
| 12 | Alex & The Star-Crossed Echoes | 98 |
| 13 | Alex & The Echoes of Eternity | 106 |
| 14 | Alex & The Nexus of Realms | 113 |
| 15 | Alex & The Healing Beyond: Astral Therapists in The New Age | 121 |
| 16 | Epilogue: Beyond the Veil - A Philosophical Closure to Astral Odysseys | 128 |
|  | About the Author | 135 |

**Dear Explorers,**

Have you ever dreamt of flying, not in an aeroplane, but with your being, soaring through skies of unimaginable colours and landscapes beyond the wildest dreams? Welcome to a brief journey into the concept of the **Astral Plane**, a realm that exists beyond the physical world we touch, see, and interact with daily.

The Astral Plane, a term you might have stumbled upon in stories of adventure and mystical exploration, is not just a fantasy. It's a concept explored by many cultures and spiritual traditions worldwide, each with its own interpretation but all agreeing on one thing: it is a place of vibrant energy, emotion, and incredible possibility.

**What is the Astral Plane?**

Imagine a layer of existence that's as real as the ground beneath your feet but operates on a different set of rules. This is the Astral Plane. It's believed to be a realm of consciousness where thoughts and emotions can take physical form, where time and space are more fluid than in our physical world. Here, you can travel to any location in the blink of an eye simply by thinking about it.

## The Magic of Astral Projection

The journey to the Astral Plane often starts with astral projection, where the conscious mind leaves the physical body and explores these other dimensions. People describe this experience as feeling a sense of profound freedom, flying across landscapes or even meeting other beings.

## A Tale of Two Friends

Let me tell you a story of Alex and Sam, two curious youngsters much like yourselves, who embarked on an unintentional journey to the Astral Plane. One quiet evening, while practising meditation in their treehouse—surrounded by the tranquil sounds of the forest and the soft glow of the setting sun—they suddenly found themselves floating.

At first, they thought it was just their imagination running wild, but soon, they realised they could see their bodies seated in meditation below them.

Panic turned into awe as they discovered they could move effortlessly through the air, passing through the treehouse's walls and soaring into the sky.

The world below them was familiar yet different. The colours were more vivid, the sounds clearer, and they felt an overwhelming sense of peace and interconnectedness with everything. They flew over mountains, dove into oceans, and even met wise beings who shared insights about the nature of reality, love, and the power of the mind.

### Lessons from the Astral Plane

Alex and Sam's adventure on the Astral Plane taught them several valuable lessons:

### *The Power of Mind:*

They learned that their thoughts and emotions could shape the reality around them, a lesson they brought back to their daily lives, understanding the importance of positivity and intention.

### *Interconnectedness:*

Their experience showed them how everything is connected at a deeper level, fostering a sense of empathy and compassion towards others and the environment.

### *The Reality Beyond Physical:*

The adventure expanded their understanding of the universe, showing them that reality is far more complex and wondrous than they had ever imagined.

### *Returning Home*

After hours of exploration, Alex and Sam felt a gentle pull back to their bodies. They opened their eyes to the familiar setting of their treehouse, the adventure on the Astral Plane now a cherished memory but leaving them forever changed.

### *Your Journey Awaits*

While Alex and Sam's journey might sound like a fantasy tale, it reminds us of the incredible potential of the human mind and spirit. The Astral Plane, seen as a literal place or a metaphor for the vastness of our inner landscape, invites us to explore beyond our physical reality's limits, learn, grow, and connect in ways we never thought possible.

So, dear explorers, I encourage you to keep an open mind and a curious heart. The world is full of mysteries waiting to be uncovered, and who knows, perhaps one day, you'll embark on your journey to the Astral Plane.

Remember, the most incredible adventures often begin with a single step—or, in the case of Alex and Sam, a leap of faith into the unknown. May your journey be filled with wonder, learning, and discovering realms beyond your own.

With an adventurous spirit,

This is **Swaminathan Murali**

[Your Guide to the Mystical and Beyond] takes you to the REALMS OF ASTRAL PLANES. Go ahead, enjoy reading and contemplate.

This note aims to demystify the concept of the Astral Plane in an engaging and accessible manner, encouraging readers to explore the vast potential of your consciousness and the universe around you.

# Prologue

## *Echoes of the Astral - A Philosophical Prelude to the Interconnected Realms*

In the fabric of existence, where the tangible meets the intangible, lies the vast expanse of the astral plane, a boundless ocean of consciousness that connects every soul, every thought, and every dream. This prologue serves as a gateway into the myriad tales of Alex and the interconnected astral realms, weaving philosophy, spirituality, and the unending quest for understanding.

## *Part 1: The Essence of the Astral Plane*

The astral plane, a realm as natural as the air we breathe yet as elusive as the wind, has long been the subject of mystics, philosophers, and seekers of truth. It is where the boundaries of time and space dissolve, and the physical and metaphysical realms converge. Plato once spoke of the realm of forms, an abstract world of perfection. The astral plane mirrors this ancient concept in many ways, serving as a canvas upon which the most profound human experiences and universal truths are painted.

## Part 2: The Thread of Consciousness

The journey into the astral realm is an inward journey that unravels the very fabric of one's being. It is here that Alex, our intrepid explorer, finds the most profound reflections of the self. The astral plane is not just a space of external exploration but an odyssey of internal discovery, echoing **Socrates's words, "An unexamined life is not worth living."**

## Part 3: The Tapestry of Interconnection

In the astral realm, every soul is interconnected, forming a vast, intricate web. This interconnectedness reflects the philosophical principle of universal oneness, where individual consciousness is part of a greater cosmic consciousness. **Rumi poetically said, "You are not a drop in the ocean. You are the entire ocean in a drop."**

## Part 4: The Duality of Existence

Much like our physical world, the astral plane is a realm of duality. It encompasses light and dark, peace and turmoil, creation and destruction. These dualities reflect the Yin and Yang of Taoist philosophy, reminding us that balance and harmony are essential in all realms of existence.

## Part 5: The Reflection of the Self

Alex's encounters in the astral realm often serve as a mirror to his inner self. Each adventure and each challenge faced reveals a layer of his psyche, offering insights into the complex nature of the human spirit. As **Carl Jung noted, "Who looks outside, dreams; who looks inside, awakes."**

## Part 6: The Nature of Time and Reality

The astral realm challenges our conventional understanding of time and reality. Past, present, and future merge, offering a nonlinear perspective of existence. This echoes **Albert Einstein's words: "The distinction between the past, present, and future is only a stubbornly persistent illusion."**

## Part 7: The Quest for Knowledge and Wisdom

Alex's journey is not just one of adventure but of enlightenment. Each foray into the astral plane is a quest for knowledge and wisdom, reflecting the age-old philosophical pursuit of understanding the mysteries of life, existence, and the cosmos.

## Part 8: The Ethical Dimensions

The astral adventures also raise ethical considerations. The realms pose questions about responsibility, the impact of actions, and the moral implications of power and knowledge. This aligns with Kant's philosophy, emphasising the importance of acting according to rules and principles.

## Part 9: The Universal and Personal Narrative

While Alex's travels in the astral plane have universal implications, they also represent a deeply personal journey. His experiences, struggles, and triumphs are a microcosm of the human condition, reflecting **Shakespeare's words, "All the world's a stage, and all the men and women merely players."**

## Part 10: The Fusion of Science and Spirituality

The astral plane stands at the crossroads of science and spirituality, merging empirical inquiry with mystical experience. It embodies the unity of these seemingly disparate realms, suggesting that the ultimate understanding of existence lies in integrating both.

## Conclusion: The Infinite Journey

As this prologue draws close, it sets the stage for a saga that transcends the ordinary, inviting readers to journey alongside Alex into the astral realms. It is an invitation to explore the mysteries of the universe and the depths of the human spirit. In the astral plane, we find answers to long-pondered questions and a reflection of our deepest selves, a reminder that within and beyond us lies an infinite expanse of possibility waiting to be explored.

In the words of the ancient philosopher Heraclitus, "No man ever steps in the same river twice, for it's not the same river, and he's not the same man." So, each journey into the astral plane is a unique passage through the ever-flowing river of consciousness. This voyage continually reshapes our understanding of reality, self, and the interconnected tapestry of existence.

# CH. 1.

# INTERCONNECTED ASTRAL REALMS

## *A Philosophical Exploration*

The concept of interconnected astral realms presents a tantalising blend of mysticism, philosophy, and speculative thought, challenging the boundaries of our understanding of reality and existence. At the heart of this idea lies the suggestion that there are realms or dimensions beyond our physical world, intricately linked and influencing each other profoundly. This essay delves into the philosophical implications of such interconnected astral realms, exploring the nature of reality, consciousness, and the potential for transcendent experiences.

### 1. The Notion of Astral Realms

The idea of astral realms is not new. It spans various cultures and periods, finding expression in ancient mythology, religious texts, and esoteric traditions. The astral realm, often conceived as a non-physical plane of existence, is thought to be populated by spirits, deities, or other non-corporeal entities. This realm is believed to be accessible through certain states of consciousness, such as dreams, meditative trances, or near-death experiences.

## 2. *Interconnectedness of Realms*

These realms' interconnectedness posits a much more complex universe than our ordinary experience suggests. It echoes the ancient Hermetic axiom, "As above, so below," implying that what happens in one realm reflects or influences occurrences in another. This idea finds some resonance in the modern concept of quantum entanglement, where particles remain connected regardless of distance, suggesting a profound underlying unity in the fabric of reality.

## 3. *Philosophical Implications*

The concept of interconnected astral realms invites several philosophical questions and implications. It challenges the materialist view of the universe as purely physical and instead suggests a more holistic, integrated understanding of existence.

## a. Nature of Reality

From a metaphysical standpoint, interconnected astral realms expand our notion of reality. If these realms exist, then reality is not just the tangible, physical world but non-material dimensions. This idea resonates with Plato's Theory of Forms, where true reality is not the material world but a realm of ideal forms. In this context, astral realms could be seen as manifestations or reflections of these ideal forms.

## b. Consciousness and Perception

Exploring astral realms often involves altered states of consciousness, raising questions about the nature and capabilities of the human mind. This brings to mind Cartesian dualism, where mind and body are distinct, and the mind can access realities beyond the physical. Furthermore, it aligns with phenomenology, emphasising the importance of subjective experience in understanding reality.

### c. Transcendence and Spiritual Experiences

Moving between different realms speaks of the human quest for transcendence, a cornerstone in many philosophical and religious traditions. This quest reflects a desire to surpass the limits of physical existence and attain a higher state of being or understanding. Mystical experiences in various religious traditions, such as the Buddhist concept of Nirvana or the Christian experience of communion with God, can be interpreted through traversing these heavenly realms.

## 4. Ethical Considerations

The notion of interconnected realms also presents ethical considerations. If our actions in the physical realm influence other realms, this implies a responsibility that extends beyond our immediate, tangible world. This concept is reminiscent of the idea of karma in Eastern philosophies, where actions have consequences across different planes of existence.

## 5. Scientific Skepticism and Interpretation

While the idea of celestial realms is rich in philosophical and mystical implications, it is met with scepticism in scientific circles. The lack of empirical evidence for such realms means they remain primarily within the domain of speculative thought. However, exploring these concepts can still offer valuable insights into human consciousness and the perennial human quest to understand the nature of reality and existence.

## 6. Astral Realms in Art and Literature

Art and literature have long explored the concept of astral realms, often as metaphors for exploring the deeper aspects of the human psyche. Works like Dante's "Divine Comedy" or Milton's "Paradise Lost" can be seen as symbolic journeys through different realms of existence, reflecting their characters' inner struggles and spiritual journeys.

## 7. Psychological and Symbolic Interpretations

From a psychological perspective, Carl Jung's concept of the collective unconscious could be seen as a symbolic astral realm. Here, archetypes and collective myths reside, influencing individual and collective psyches. This approach suggests that astral realms may not be literal places but symbolic landscapes of the human mind.

## 8. Integration with Holistic Worldviews

The concept of interconnected astral realms aligns well with holistic and integrative worldviews, such as those found in certain New Age philosophies and some interpretations of quantum physics. These perspectives emphasise the interconnectedness and interdependence of all things, blurring the lines between physical and non-physical science and spirituality.

## 9. Personal and Societal Transformation

On a personal level, the belief in astral realms can lead to transformative experiences, offering new ways of understanding oneself and the world. On a societal level, it can foster a sense of unity and interconnectedness, countering the often fragmented and materialistic worldview prevalent in contemporary society.

## 10. The Future of Astral Realm Exploration

As humanity continues to evolve technologically and spiritually, exploring concepts like astral realms may take new forms. Whether through advancements in neuroscience, virtual reality technologies, or more profound spiritual practices, the quest to understand and experience these realms will likely continue to captivate the human imagination.

## *Conclusion*

The concept of interconnected heavenly realms, while largely speculative and beyond the purview of empirical science, offers a rich field for philosophical exploration. It challenges us to expand our understanding of reality, to reconsider the nature of consciousness and perception, and to reflect on the ethical dimensions of our actions across possible multiple dimensions of existence. Whether these realms are literal or metaphorical, their exploration can provide valuable insights into the human condition and our place in the cosmos. As we ponder these mysteries, we keep alive the age-old human quest for knowledge and understanding, a testament to the depth and reach of the human spirit.

# CH. 2.

# ASTRAL PROJECTION AS A COMMON SKILL:

# A PHILOSOPHICAL NARRATIVE

In a world where astral projection is not a mystical rarity but an ordinary skill, the fabric of society and the individual's understanding of existence undergo profound transformations. This narrative explores such a world, interweaving philosophical musings within a story of discovery and self-realisation.

## Part 1: The Awakening

In the city of Eudaimonia, astral projection was as ordinary as breathing. People routinely slipped out of their physical forms to explore, learn, and connect in ways beyond physical limitations. This ability, however, was not just a means of escape but a path to deeper understanding and communal harmony.

Amidst this city lived Alex, a young individual with an insatiable curiosity about the nature of this ability and its implications. Alex often wondered, "If we can separate our consciousness from our physical body, what does this say about the nature of our existence?"

## Part 2: The Philosophical Journey

Alex's quest for understanding led to late nights spent in the Great Library of Eudaimonia, poring over texts that ranged from ancient philosophy to modern theoretical physics. The writings of Plato, discussing the realm of forms and the idea that actual reality was beyond physical perception, resonated deeply with Alex. If astral projection allowed one to experience a realm beyond the physical, was this not akin to accessing Plato's world of forms?

Moreover, Alex delved into Descartes' meditations, contemplating the separation of mind and body. This duality seemed to manifest literally in their world, where one's consciousness could exist independently of physical form. But unlike Descartes, who doubted the external world to prove his existence, Alex and fellow Eudaimonians used astral projection to connect more deeply with the external reality, both physical and beyond.

## Part 3: The Experiment

Determined to explore these philosophical concepts through experience, Alex embarked on an experiment. They would use astral projection not just for exploration but as a method to understand the interconnectedness of all things. This idea mirrored the Eastern philosophies of interdependence and oneness.

During these astral journeys, Alex encountered diverse minds and realms. Some realms were abstract landscapes of pure thought and emotion, while others mirrored the physical world, revealing its deeper, hidden connections. Alex started to document these experiences, finding parallels in Jung's concept of the collective unconscious.

### *Part 4: The Revelation*

One night, during a particularly profound projection, Alex found themselves in a realm of luminous interconnectedness, where every thought and emotion had a colour and sound, creating a symphony of consciousness. Here, Alex encountered Sophia, an elder who deeply understood astral realms.

Sophia shared with Alex the ancient philosophy of Anima Mundi, the belief in a world soul. "In our projections," she explained, "we not only explore different realms but also connect with this world soul, experiencing the unity of all existence."

This revelation struck a chord with Alex. Astral projection wasn't just about individual exploration or escape; it was a tool for understanding the intrinsic connectedness of all beings.

## *Part 5: The Ethical Awakening*

With this new understanding, Alex began to ponder the ethical implications. If everyone was interconnected, then each action, thought, and emotion in both physical and heavenly realms had ripple effects. This resonated with the concept of karma in Eastern philosophy, suggesting a moral responsibility transcending physical existence.

## *Part 6: The Community*

As Alex shared these insights with others, a transformation began in Eudaimonia. Astral projection, once seen as an individualistic endeavour, became a communal journey towards greater understanding and empathy. People started to use this skill for personal growth, resolving conflicts, deepening compassion, and fostering a sense of global community.

## Part 7: The Challenge

However, this shift was challenging. Some sceptics viewed astral projection merely as escapism to avoid dealing with the tangible world's problems. Alex and their like-minded peers faced the task of integrating their astral experiences into concrete actions, improving their lives and society.

## Part 8: The Integration

This integration led to a renaissance in Eudaimonia. Science, art, and philosophy advances flourished as people drew inspiration from physical and astral experiences. The city became a beacon of progress and harmony, a testament to the potential of humanity when it embraced its full capabilities.

## Part 9: The Personal Transformation

Throughout this journey, Alex underwent a profound personal transformation. They realised that astral projection was a skill and a pathway to wisdom. It was a means to transcend the ego, to experience the interconnectedness of existence, and to bring back insights that could transform the physical world.

## Part 10: The Legacy

Years later, Alex, now a mentor to others, reflected on the journey. They had started with questions about the nature of reality and existence and found profoundly simple and infinitely complex answers. The astral projection was not just about exploring other realms but a tool for understanding the self and the universe.

## *Conclusion*

In the story of Eudaimonia and Alex, astral projection as an ordinary skill becomes a powerful metaphor for the human capacity for transcendence, connection, and understanding. It challenges us to think deeply about the nature of our existence, the potential of our consciousness, and our responsibilities towards each other. This narrative, blending philosophy with imaginative storytelling, invites us to consider the possibilities within and beyond us in our continuous quest for knowledge and meaning in the vast tapestry of existence.

## CH. 3.

# THE ODYSSEY OF ALEX:

# A PHILOSOPHICAL JOURNEY BEYOND THE ASTRAL

In the bustling metropolis of Eudaimonia, where the art of astral projection had woven itself into the fabric of daily life, Alex embarked on a journey that transcended the physical realm, venturing deep into the terrains of philosophy, consciousness, and the human spirit.

### Part 1: The Inner Voyage

Having mastered the art of astral projection, Alex had always felt a profound connection with Socrates' words: *"An unexamined life is not worth living."* This philosophical mantra became the compass of their journey, guiding them through the heavenly realms and the labyrinth of their psyche.

### Part 2: The Quest for Wisdom

In the realm of Eudaimonia, wisdom was not merely acquired; it was lived. For Alex, this pursuit of wisdom transcended the conventional −a journey that blurred the lines between the physical and the metaphysical. As they delved deeper into philosophical texts, they encountered the words of Lao Tzu: *"The journey of a thousand miles begins with one step."* These words resonated with Alex, reminding them that each astral journey, each philosophical inquiry, was a step towards a deeper understanding of the universe and themselves.

## Part 3: The Ethereal Classroom

During their astral travels, Alex often visited the Ethereal Classroom, where thinkers from different epochs gathered. Here, dialogues were not bound by time or space – Plato debated with Nietzsche, and Confucius exchanged ideas with Kant. In this transcendent academy, Alex realised the fluidity of knowledge and the interconnectedness of all ideas.

## Part 4: The Nature of Reality

One night, under the astral skies, Alex pondered the words of Albert Einstein: *"Reality is merely an illusion, albeit a very persistent one."* This statement challenged their understanding of the physical world. Was the reality experienced during astral projection any less accurate, or was it a different facet of the same cosmic diamond of existence?

## *Part 5: The Duality of Being*

Alex's explorations led them to contemplate the duality of their existence – the physical and the astral. This duality echoed Descartes's philosophical musings and his cogito ergo sum (I think, therefore I am). But in Alex's experience, it was not just thought that affirmed existence but also the ability to transcend physicality and explore other realms of being.

## *Part 6: The Ethical Dimension*

As their understanding deepened, Alex grappled with the ethical implications of their actions, both in the physical and astral planes. They were reminded of Kant's categorical imperative, which urged actions that could be willed into universal law. This principle gained new dimensions in astral interactions, where thoughts and intentions could have tangible effects.

## *Part 7: The Symphony of Emotions*

During one astral venture, Alex experienced what they could only describe as a symphony of emotions, a harmonious blend of feelings and thoughts that transcended language. It vividly embodied Spinoza's idea that *"nothing can be destroyed except through an external cause."* This unity of emotions in the astral realm revealed the indestructibility and interconnectedness of the emotional and intellectual human experience.

## *Part 8: The Paradox of Freedom*

In their philosophical musings, Alex often reflected on the concept of freedom. The astral realms offered a kind of liberation from physical constraints, yet the limits of their consciousness also bounded this freedom. It brought to mind Jean-Paul Sartre's assertion that *"freedom is what you do with what's been done to you."* Alex realised that true freedom lay in the choices made in the astral and physical worlds.

## Part 9: The Return to Self

Each astral journey brought Alex back to themselves, leading to a deeper self-realisation. Like the words of Rumi, *"What you seek is seeking you,"* Alex understood that their quest for knowledge and understanding was also a journey towards self-discovery. Each projection became a mirror reflecting their innermost being.

## Part 10: The Legacy of Knowledge

In their later years, Alex, now a sage in their own right, pondered the legacy of their journeys. They realised that the most incredible wisdom they could impart was the importance of questioning and seeking. *"The only true wisdom is in knowing you know nothing,"* Socrates said, which echoed through Alex's teachings. They encouraged others to embark on their journeys, whether through astral projection or exploring the vast realms of philosophy.

## *Conclusion*

Alex's astral and philosophical journey was a testament to the unquenchable human thirst for knowledge and understanding. Their life, a tapestry woven from threads of metaphysical experiences and deep philosophical insights, stood as a beacon to all who sought to explore beyond the visible horizons. In the story of Alex, we find not just an exploration of astral realms but a profound narrative about the quest for wisdom, the nature of reality, and the eternal dance between the physical and the metaphysical. This journey, rich in introspection and discovery, reminds us that pursuing knowledge is an endless odyssey, where each answer unlocks new questions, and every journey inward reveals the universe within us.

# CH. 4.

# ASTRAL DETECTIVES:

# THE UNSEEN THREADS OF REALITY

In the heart of Eudaimonia, where astral projection was as standard as the bustling street markets, a unique group of individuals harnessed this skill for a noble purpose. They were the Astral Detectives, unravelling mysteries and solving crimes by traversing the unseen layers of reality. Among them was Alex, whose philosophical mind and mastery of astral travel made them an invaluable team member.

### Part 1: The Invisible Crime

The case began with a mystery that baffled even the most seasoned investigators in Eudaimonia. A valuable artefact had vanished from the Museum of Ancient History with no signs of break-in or disturbance. The physical evidence was scant, but the Astral Detectives knew that clues might lie beyond the tangible realm.

### Part 2: The Astral Investigation

As they embarked on their astral journey, Alex recalled the words of Heraclitus: "Nature loves to hide." This truth was never more evident than in the astral realm, where secrets concealed in the physical world lay bare to those who could perceive them.

## *Part 3: The Realm of Echoes*

Their first stop was the Realm of Echoes, an astral plane where past events resonated like whispers. Here, time folded upon itself, allowing the detectives to witness echoes of the theft. They saw not the thief's physical form but the emotional and mental imprints left behind – a trail of greed, cunning, and fear.

## *Part 4: The Web of Connections*

The clues from the Realm of Echoes led them to the Web of Connections, a plane where the relationships between people and objects were visible as luminous threads. Alex, reflecting on the Buddhist teaching of Pratītyasamutpāda or dependent origination, understood that every event was interconnected. In this web, they traced the stolen artefact's journey across the city, each thread a story of its own.

## Part 5: The Veil of Illusions

Their next destination was the Veil of Illusions, a realm where the mind's deceptions often obscured the true nature of things. It reminded Alex of Plato's Allegory of the Cave, where we perceive mere shadows of reality. Here, they had to discern the truth amidst the myriad illusions, which tested their wisdom and insight.

## Part 6: The Encounter with the Shadow

In the depths of the astral plane, Alex encountered the thief's shadow self, a manifestation of their subconscious guilt and fear. Drawing on Carl Jung's concepts, Alex engaged in a dialogue with this shadow, unravelling the psychological motives behind the crime. This encounter revealed not only the whereabouts of the artefact but also the thief's deep-seated reasons for the theft.

## *Part 7: The Ethical Dilemma*

However, the case resolution brought an ethical dilemma to the forefront. The detectives could easily expose the thief with their astral findings, but Alex pondered the moral implications. Nietzsche's words echoed in their mind: "Whoever fights monsters should see to it that in the process, he does not become a monster." They grappled with the responsibility that came with their unique abilities – the balance between justice and compassion.

## *Part 8: The Resolution*

The team decided to confront the thief in the physical world, armed with the understanding gained from their astral investigation. They offered a chance for redemption, appealing to the thief's conscience. The stolen artefact was returned, and the thief, moved by the detectives' empathy, sought a new path.

## Part 9: The Reflection

In the aftermath, Alex reflected on the case, contemplating Gandhi's words: "The true measure of any society can be found in how it treats its most vulnerable members." They realised that their role as a cosmic detective was not just to solve crimes but to heal the rifts in society, to bring to light the unseen struggles and pains that often led to such transgressions.

## Part 10: The Legacy

Years later, Alex, now a mentor to aspiring astral detectives, taught not only the techniques of astral travel but also the philosophy behind their work. They emphasised the importance of understanding, compassion, and ethical responsibility. The Astral Detectives had become more than mere investigators; they were guardians of the delicate balance between the seen and unseen, the physical and the metaphysical.

## *Conclusion*

The story of the Astral Detectives, with Alex at its heart, weaves a narrative that transcends the conventional bounds of detective work. It delves into the philosophical implications of accessing unseen realms and the ethical responsibilities of such power. Through their adventures, we are reminded of the complex tapestry of human existence, where every action, thought, and emotion is interconnected. This tale invites us to ponder justice, truth, and our place in the vast, mysterious universe.

# CH. 5.

## ALEX'S ODYSSEY:

## THE ASTRAL MIRROR OF THE SOUL

Alex embarked on a profound journey of self-discovery in the mystical city of Eudaimonia, where the astral realm was as familiar as the winding streets. Here, the astral plane was not just a separate universe but a reflection of one's inner consciousness. Each journey into this ethereal realm became a deep dive into the psyche, revealing the most intimate landscapes of the soul.

### Part 1: The Genesis of the Journey

Alex, now a sage in both the physical and astral worlds, understood that to navigate the complexities of the human soul, one must first journey inward. They remembered the words of *Carl Jung: "Who looks outside, dreams; who looks inside, awakes."* It was this awakening that Alex sought in the astral plane.

### Part 2: The Mirror of the Mind

As Alex entered their astral realm, they found themselves in a vast, ever-changing landscape. It was a world that mirrored their thoughts, fears, dreams, and desires. The terrain shifted with the tides of their emotions, a visual symphony of their subconscious mind.

### Part 3: The Valley of Shadows

The first terrain Alex encountered was the Valley of Shadows, where their fears and insecurities loomed large. Here, they faced the embodiment of their deepest anxieties, confronting them with the courage of Odysseus facing the Cyclops. This was a trial by fire, a necessary passage through the dark night of the soul.

### Part 4: The River of Reflection

Emerging from the Valley, Alex came upon the River of Reflection, a tranquil stream that mirrored their true self. As they gazed into the water, they saw their physical form and the essence of their being. It was a moment of introspection, guided by the words of *Socrates: "To know thyself is the beginning of wisdom."*

## *Part 5: The Forest of Forgiveness*

Beyond the river lay the Forest of Forgiveness, a serene space where Alex confronted past mistakes and regrets. Each tree in the forest represented a moment of choice, a reminder of paths taken and not taken. In this forest, Alex learned to forgive themselves, understanding that, as *Alexander Pope wrote, "To err is human, to forgive, divine."*

## *Part 6: The Mountain of Aspirations*

Alex's journey led them to the Mountain of Aspirations, a towering peak representing their highest hopes and ambitions. Climbing this mountain was a metaphor for their personal growth and pursuing their life's purpose. *The words of Thoreau rang true here: "What you get by achieving your goals is not as important as what you become by achieving your goals."*

## *Part 7: The Sanctuary of Love*

At the heart of the astral realm was the Sanctuary of Love, a space of profound emotional connections. Here, Alex experienced the full spectrum of love – from the love of family and friends to the universal love for all beings. It was a realisation of *Bell Hooks' words: "Love is an action, never simply a feeling."*

## Part 8: The Hall of Mirrors

In the Hall of Mirrors, Alex encountered various versions of themselves – each reflecting a different aspect of their personality. This was a journey through the many selves, an exploration of the multifaceted nature of their identity. Alex truly understood *Walt Whitman's line, "I contain multitudes."*

## Part 9: The Return to Oneness

At the culmination of the journey, Alex found themselves in a realm of pure light, where all distinctions dissolved into a state of oneness. It was an experience of the unity of all existence, a moment of enlightenment where the words of *Rumi echoed: "You are not a drop in the ocean. You are the entire ocean in a drop."*

## *Part 10: The Wisdom Gained*

Returning from the astral journey, Alex brought back personal insights and a deeper understanding of the human condition. They realised that every person's astral realm was a unique universe, a sacred space for healing, growth, and self-realisation.

## *Conclusion*

Alex's astral odyssey was more than a journey through ethereal landscapes; it explored the innermost depths of the soul. In this journey, they uncovered the intricate tapestry of their being, gaining wisdom and compassion. This narrative serves as a reminder of the boundless potential for growth and discovery within us. In the astral mirror, we confront our shadows, embrace our light, and emerge with a deeper understanding of ourselves and our place in the cosmos.

## CH. 6.

# ALEX AND THE LABYRINTH OF TIME:

# AN ASTRAL ODYSSEY

In the mystical realms of Eudaimonia, where the boundaries of reality were as malleable as clay, Alex, a seasoned astral traveller, embarked on an extraordinary journey through the labyrinth of time. The astral plane, a boundless expanse beyond physical time and space constraints, offered a unique perspective on the past, present, and future.

## Part 1: The Enigma of Time

As Alex delved into the astral realm, they were immediately struck by its peculiar relationship with time. Time was not a linear stream but a vast ocean with currents flowing in all directions. It brought to mind *Einstein's words: "The distinction between the past, present, and future is only a stubbornly persistent illusion."*

## Part 2: The Tapestry of History

Alex's first encounter in this temporal odyssey was with the Tapestry of History, a visual representation of the past where each thread represented a moment. As they touched each thread, they experienced moments from history, realising the interconnectedness of all events. It vividly illustrated *William Faulkner's assertion: "The past is never dead. It's not even past."*

### Part 3: The Garden of Forking Paths

Venturing further, Alex found themselves in the Garden of Forking Paths, a symbol of the present where every decision branched into many possibilities. Here, they saw the immediate impact of choices, understanding the profound truth in *Robert Frost's words: "Two roads diverged in a wood, and I— I took the one less travelled by, And that has made all the difference."*

### Part 4: The River of Futures

Next, Alex navigated the River of Futures, a fluid and ever-changing stream showing the myriad potential futures. This was a place of dreams and visions, each ripple representing a possible outcome.

The experience resonated with the words of *T.S. Eliot: "Time present and time past are both perhaps present in time future, and time future contained in time past."*

## Part 5: The Echoes of Consequence

In the astral plane, Alex also discovered the Echoes of Consequence, a realm where the long-term effects of actions were felt. Here, they realised the weight of their decisions, seeing how each choice rippled through time, impacting generations. This brought a sense of responsibility and echoed the philosophical notion of Karma – the law of cause and effect.

## Part 6: The Dilemma of Intervention

As Alex delved deeper into the mysteries of time, they faced a moral dilemma: the possibility of altering the past or influencing the future. The temptation was immense, but so were the potential consequences. They recalled the words of *Kierkegaard: "Life can only be understood backwards, but it must be lived forwards."* The decision to intervene or not became a profound ethical quandary.

### Part 7: The Paradox of Predestination

Alex explored the Paradox of Predestination, where fate and free will intertwine. Were their actions predestined, or were they the master of their destiny? This conundrum reflected the age-old philosophical debate, encapsulated in the words of *Jean-Paul Sartre: "We are our choices."*

### Part 8: The Sphere of Infinite Possibilities

In the Sphere of Infinite Possibilities, Alex realised that every moment was a nexus of infinite potentialities. It was a revelation that every second held limitless possibilities, a concept beautifully expressed by Jorge Luis Borges in his labyrinthine stories. This realisation empowered Alex with a deeper appreciation of the present moment.

## Part 9: The Wisdom of Temporal Acceptance

After traversing the complexities of the astral time, Alex emerged with a profound understanding of the temporal nature of existence. They learned to embrace the flow of time, understanding that each moment was a precious gift not to be squandered. It echoed the words of *Marcus Aurelius: "Time is a sort of river of passing events, and strong is its current; no sooner is a thing brought to sight than it is swept by and another takes its place, and this too will be swept away."*

## Part 10: The Return to the Present

Alex returned to the physical world with a deeper understanding of time and a renewed sense of purpose. They realised that while they could explore the past and future, living in the present was where true meaning lay. It was an acknowledgement of the power of now, a concept espoused by Eckhart Tolle and other spiritual teachers.

## *Conclusion*

Alex's journey through the astral plane of time was a profound exploration of fate, destiny, and the consequences of tampering with the fabric of time. It was a narrative that intertwined philosophy, ethics, and the mysteries of existence. Through this odyssey, Alex, and in turn, the readers, are reminded of the intricate dance of time and how our actions and decisions weave and tune our lives. Ultimately, the astral plane offered insights into the mysteries of time and lessons on living a meaningful, present-focused life.

# CH. 7.

# ALEX AND THE SHADOWS OF THE ASTRAL:

# A COSMIC BALANCE IN PERIL

A new, unprecedented threat emerged in the mystical city of Eudaimonia, where astral travel was as commonplace as walking. This menace, an evil force, began to distort and endanger the astral realms. Alex, a seasoned astral traveller and sage, was drawn into a quest to neutralise this threat, a journey that would test their wisdom, courage, and understanding of the cosmos.

## Part 1: The Emergence of the Threat

The disruption began subtly, with astral travellers reporting disorienting experiences, landscapes in the astral realm twisting into nightmarish versions of themselves. Alex, sensing a disturbance in the cosmic balance, recalled the words of *Heraclitus: "The only constant in life is change."* They knew that this change was a harbinger of something deeply unsettling.

## Part 2: The Shadow Entity

Alex's investigation led them to encounter the Shadow Entity, a dark force that fed on the fear and negative energy of astral beings. This entity threatened to consume the astral planes, turning them into realms of despair. *Jung's* words resonated with Alex: *"Everyone carries a shadow, and the less it is embodied in the individual's conscious life, the blacker and denser it is."*

## Part 3: The Imbalance of Energies

Delving deeper, Alex realised that the Shadow Entity was a manifestation of a cosmic imbalance. The astral planes were realms of equilibrium, where light and dark and positive and negative energies coexisted. This entity was tipping the scales, threatening the very fabric of the astral realms. It echoed the *Taoist philosophy of Yin and Yang, the balance of opposing forces.*

## Part 4: The Quest for the Ancient Artifacts

To neutralise the threat, Alex embarked on a quest to gather ancient artefacts, each imbued with the power to restore balance. This journey took them across various astral realms, each reflecting the diverse aspects of existence. It was a quest reminiscent of Joseph Campbell's Hero's Journey, where the protagonist must undergo trials to restore harmony.

## Part 5: The Ethereal Guardians

Alex encountered Ethereal Guardians in each realm, astral beings who protected the artefacts. These guardians challenged Alex not with brute force but with philosophical dilemmas and moral quandaries. It was a test of wisdom and ethics, reflecting Plato's belief in pursuing virtue and knowledge.

## Part 6: The Convergence of Realms

As Alex collected the artefacts, the convergence of realms began, a phenomenon where the boundaries between different astral planes blurred. This convergence was both a challenge and an opportunity, allowing Alex to harness the combined energies of the realms. It was a cosmic alignment that reflected the interconnectedness of all things, a concept central to Buddhist philosophy.

### Part 7: The Ritual of Restoration

Alex performed the Ritual of Restoration with the artefacts in hand, a complex ceremony that required a deep understanding of astral energies. The ritual was a delicate balance of channelling and containing the energies, a task that reminded Alex of the words of *Nikola Tesla: "If you want to find the secrets of the universe, think in terms of energy, frequency, and vibration."*

### Part 8: The Dissolution of the Shadow Entity

As the ritual climaxed, the Shadow Entity fought back, a storm of dark energy clashing with the light. In this crisis, Alex realised that the entity could not be destroyed but must be integrated and understood. It was a profound insight, reflecting Carl Jung's concept of integrating the shadow self.

## Part 9: The Restoration of Balance

The ritual succeeded, and the astral planes were restored to their natural state of equilibrium. Now understood and acknowledged, the Shadow Entity ceased to be a destructive force and became a part of the cosmic balance. Alex had not only saved the astral realms but had also brought a deeper understanding of the duality of existence.

## Part 10: The Wisdom Gained

Returning from their journey, Alex brought back a renewed sense of the delicate balance of the cosmos. They understood that darkness and light were not adversaries but complementary forces. It was a lesson in the acceptance and understanding of all aspects of existence, a realisation of the words of *Rumi: "The wound is the place where the Light enters you."*

## *Conclusion*

Alex's adventure against the Shadows of the Astral was more than a battle against an external threat; it was a journey into the depths of cosmic understanding and self-realisation. This narrative explores the philosophy of balance, the integration of opposites, and the importance of understanding one's shadow self. The story is a metaphor for our internal battles and the importance of confronting and integrating our darker aspects to achieve personal and universal harmony.

## CH. 8.

# ALEX AND THE GUARDIANS OF THE ASTRAL:

# A QUEST FOR COSMIC CONSERVATION

A new challenge arose in the mystical realms of Eudaimonia, where astral travel was a bridge between worlds. Once vibrant and harmonious, the astral planes began showing signs of distress. This disturbance was attributed to irresponsible astral travel by novices and thrill-seekers. Alex, now a guardian of the astral ecology, embarked on a mission to restore balance and educate others about the importance of astral conservation.

### *Part 1: The Fragility of the Astral Ecosystem*

Alex first noticed the changes during their routine travels. The once luminous astral flora began to wilt, and the ethereal fauna appeared disoriented. The astral realms, they realised, were not immune to harm. This revelation was a stark reminder *of Chief Seattle's words: "Man does not weave the web of life; he is merely a strand in it. Whatever he does to the web, he does to himself."*

## Part 2: The Cause of the Imbalance

Investigation revealed that the influx of inexperienced travellers, who navigated the astral planes with little regard for their delicate nature, was causing the imbalance. Their reckless energy left a trail of disruption akin to footprints too heavy on a path less travelled. It brought to mind *Rachel Carson's warning: "Man's attitude toward nature is today critically important simply because we have now acquired a fateful power to alter and destroy nature."*

## Part 3: The Formation of the Astral Conservation Corps

Realising the urgency, Alex formed the Astral Conservation Corps, a group dedicated to protecting and preserving the astral ecology. The corps comprised experienced astral travellers, sages, and even enlightened beings from various realms. Their mission echoed the words of *Aldo Leopold: "A thing is right when it tends to preserve the integrity, stability, and beauty of the biotic community. It is wrong when it tends otherwise."*

## Part 4: The Education Initiative

Alex and the Corps began educating new astral travellers about the importance of responsible travel. Workshops, guided journeys, and mentorship programs were established, emphasising the astral realm's need for harmony and respect. *The philosophy of Socrates guided this educational initiative: "Wisdom begins in wonder."*

## Part 5: Healing the Astral Wounds

The Corps undertook missions to heal the astral damage. This involved complex rituals, restoring energies, and nurturing the astral fauna and flora back to health. The slow process required patience and a deep understanding of astral mechanics. It was a testament to the words of *Jane Goodall: "You cannot get through a single day without having an impact on the world around you. What you do makes a difference, and you must decide what kind of difference you want to make."*

## Part 6: The Implementation of Astral Regulations

The Corps implemented astral travel regulations to prevent further harm, setting guidelines for sustainable exploration. These regulations were not restrictions but measures to ensure that the beauty and sanctity of the astral planes were preserved for future generations. It reflected the ethos of *Gifford Pinchot: "Conservation means the wise use of the earth and its resources for the lasting good of men."*

## Part 7: The Astral Sanctuary Zones

Particular areas within the astral realm were designated as sanctuary zones, places of healing and refuge for its inhabitants. These zones were free from human interference, allowing the astral ecosystem to thrive naturally. The creation of these sanctuaries was a nod to John *Muir's belief: "When we try to pick out anything by itself, we find it hitched to everything else in the Universe."*

## Part 8: The Ripple Effect

The efforts of Alex and the Corps began to show positive results. The astral realm started rejuvenating, and its natural harmony was slowly restored. This success had a ripple effect, encouraging travellers to adopt a more respectful approach to astral exploration. It was a real-world application of the butterfly effect, where small changes could lead to significant impacts.

## Part 9: The Philosophy of Coexistence

Alex developed a more profound philosophy of coexistence through this journey, not just in the astral realm but in all aspects of life. They understood that every action, physical or astral, had consequences, and living in harmony with all realms was crucial for the balance of the cosmos. This understanding was beautifully encapsulated in the words of *Albert Einstein: "Look deep into nature, and then you will understand everything better."*

## Part 10: The Legacy of the Astral Guardians

Alex and the Astral Conservation Corps left a lasting legacy in restoring the astral realm and instilling a sense of responsibility and ethics in astral travel. Their journey was a reminder of the interconnectedness of all existence and the importance of preserving the delicate balance of the cosmos.

# *Conclusion*

The story of Alex and the Guardians of the Astral serves as a metaphor for environmental conservation and the impact of human actions on both the physical and non-physical realms. It emphasises the need for responsibility, education, and respect in all interactions with nature, echoing the belief that preserving the world's natural beauty and balance is a shared responsibility. This narrative invites readers to reflect on their relationship with the natural world and the legacy they wish to leave for future generations.

## CH. 9.

# ALEX AND THE TAPESTRY OF TIME:

# UNRAVELING THE ASTRAL THREADS OF CULTURES

In the cosmopolitan city of Eudaimonia, astral projection was not merely a skill but a tapestry woven with the threads of various cultures and historical epochs. Alex, an adept astral traveller, embarked on a journey to explore these diverse astral traditions, uncovering a world rich in history, culture, and philosophy.

## Part 1: The Ancient Egyptian Realms

Alex's journey began in the astral realms of Ancient Egypt, where astral projection was intertwined with their beliefs in the afterlife. The Egyptians viewed the astral plane as a Duat, a realm where souls journeyed after death. In this realm, Alex marvelled at the vibrant astral hieroglyphs depicting the soul's journey, echoing *Hermes Trismegistus's words: "As above, so below, as within, so without, as the universe, so the soul."*

## *Part 2: The Greek Philosophers' Domain*

Next, Alex visited the astral realms influenced by ancient Greek philosophy. Here, astral projection was a method of attaining higher knowledge, akin to Plato's theory of forms. In this realm, Alex engaged in debates with the astral forms of Socrates and Aristotle, pondering the nature of reality. It was a living manifestation of *Aristotle's saying: "Knowing yourself is the beginning of all wisdom."*

## *Part 3: The Shamanic Spirits of Indigenous Cultures*

Venturing into the astral landscapes of indigenous cultures, Alex encountered shamanic realms. Astral travel was a sacred communion with spirit guides and ancestors. In their astral form, the shamans taught Alex about the interconnectedness of all life, reflecting the words of *Chief Seattle: "All things are connected like the blood that unites us all."*

## Part 4: The Eastern Mystics' Enlightenment

In the astral realms influenced by Eastern mysticism, Alex discovered a serene landscape where astral projection was a path to enlightenment. In these realms, the concepts of karma and dharma were intricately woven into the fabric of astral travel. It was a direct experience of the *Buddha's teaching: "Do not dwell in the past, do not dream of the future, concentrate the mind on the present moment."*

## Part 5: The Medieval European Astral Realms

Alex then found themselves in the astral realms shaped by medieval European alchemists and mystics. Here, astral projection was often cloaked in secrecy, intertwined with the search for spiritual gold. The esoteric symbols and alchemical processes in this realm were a direct reflection of the saying of *Paracelsus: "The art of healing comes from nature, not from the physician."*

## Part 6: The Vibrant African Astral Lands

In the astral realms influenced by African cultures, Alex discovered a vibrant world where astral projection was integral to community and storytelling. These realms were filled with the rhythms of ancestral drums and the wisdom of oral traditions, embodying the *African proverb: "Wisdom does not come overnight."*

## Part 7: The Native American Spirit Walks

In the realms echoing Native American traditions, astral projection was a spirit walk, a journey for guidance and healing. Alex encountered astral landscapes of vast prairies and learned from the spirit animals. It was a living example of the *Native American saying: "We do not inherit the earth from our ancestors; we borrow it from our children."*

## Part 8: The Mesmerizing Sufi Whirling Realms

Alex experienced the mesmerising dance of the Sufi dervishes in the astral realms inspired by Sufism. Astral projection was a meditation, a whirling dance leading to divine love and truth. Alex realised the essence of *Rumi's words: "You are not a drop in the ocean. You are the entire ocean in a drop."*

## Part 9: The Modern Metaphysical Movements

Finally, Alex explored the astral realms shaped by modern metaphysical movements. Here, astral projection blended with new-age philosophies and technological advancements. It was a realm where the ancient and the modern coexisted, reflecting the quote by *Carl Sagan: "Science is not only compatible with spirituality; it is a profound source of spirituality."*

## Part 10: The Integration of Astral Wisdom

Returning from this grand voyage across time and culture, Alex realised that each culture's astral tradition was a unique interpretation of a universal experience. This journey was not just about understanding different cultures but about seeing the interconnectedness of human experience through the lens of astral travel. It vividly embodied *William Blake's vision: "To see a world in a grain of sand and a heaven in a wild flower, hold infinity in the palm of your hand, and eternity in an hour."*

## *Conclusion*

Alex's exploration of the diverse cultural and historical interpretations of astral projection is a rich tapestry, illustrating the multitude of ways humanity has sought to understand and navigate the astral realm. This narrative not only enriches the world-building of Eudaimonia but also offers a deeper insight into the human spirit's quest for knowledge, connection, and transcendence. Through this journey, Alex and the readers are reminded that while cultures may vary in their expressions and understanding of the astral, the core human yearning for exploration and comprehension of the unknown is a universal trait that binds us all.

# CH. 10.

# ALEX AND THE ECHOES OF THE ASTRAL WAR

In the realm of Eudaimonia, the astral plane was a space of exploration and discovery and a battleground where unseen wars were fought. These conflicts, mirroring the struggles of the physical world or born of unique astral disputes, painted a complex tapestry of harmony and discord. Alex, now a seasoned traveller of the astral realm, found themselves amid these tumultuous battles, where astral warriors wielded magic and engaged in combat that defied the laws of the physical world.

## Part 1: The Awakening to Conflict

Alex first became aware of the astral conflicts during a routine journey. They stumbled upon a skirmish between two factions, each fighting for their ideologies and spiritual dominion. This encounter resonated with Sun *Tzu's philosophy: "The supreme art of war is to subdue the enemy without fighting."*

## Part 2: The Nature of Astral Warfare

Unlike physical battles, astral warfare was a clash of energies, intentions, and wills. Warriors in the astral plane battled with manifestations of their inner strength, wielding weapons that were extensions of their spiritual essence. *Carl von Clausewitz noted, "War is the realm of uncertainty; three-quarters of the factors on which action is based are wrapped in a fog of greater or lesser uncertainty."*

## Part 3: The Ethereal Art of Combat

Astral combat was an art form, a dance of consciousness transcending physical constraints. Here, the strength of a warrior lies in their ability to harness and direct astral energy. Alex learned to engage in these battles, recalling *Miyamoto Musashi's words: "The way of the warrior is resolute acceptance of death."*

## Part 4: Reflections of Earthly Conflicts

Some astral battles reflected earthly conflicts, where humanity's collective emotions and thoughts shaped the astral landscape. These battles were intense, fueled by the passions and turmoil of the physical world. Alex realised the truth in *George Orwell's observation: "All war is a symptom of man's failure as a thinking animal."*

## Part 5: The Unique Astral Disputes

Other conflicts in the astral realm were unique to its nature, often revolving around the balance of astral energies and the protection of its sanctuaries. These disputes required a deep understanding of astral mechanics and the delicate balance of cosmic forces. In these battles, Alex remembered the words of A*lbert Einstein: "Peace cannot be kept by force; it can only be achieved by understanding."*

## Part 6: The Role of the Astral Warriors

Astral warriors, like Alex, often served as protectors of the realm's equilibrium. They were guardians who sought to maintain or restore peace, understanding the responsibility that came with their power. This role was a living embodiment of the *Spiderman principle: "With great power comes great responsibility."*

## Part 7: The Magic of the Astral

Magic in the astral realm was a tangible force, an energy wielded by the warriors in their struggles. This magic was diverse, ranging from elemental powers to the manipulation of astral landscapes. Alex learned to harness this magic, echoing *Arthur C. Clarke's third law: "Any sufficiently advanced technology is indistinguishable from magic."*

## Part 8: The Impact on the Physical World

The outcomes of astral battles often had ripples in the physical world, influencing events in subtle but significant ways. Alex understood the interconnectedness of both realms and the consequences of their actions, reflecting on *J.R.R. Tolkien's insight: "The deeds that move the wheels of the world may be attempted by the smallest."*

## Part 9: The Path to Resolution

In seeking resolutions to these conflicts, Alex often engaged in diplomacy as much as combat. They understood that true victory in the astral plane was not the defeat of an opponent but the restoration of balance and harmony. This wisdom was captured in *Nelson Mandela's words: "Peace is not just the absence of conflict; peace is the creation of an environment where all can flourish."*

## *Part 10: The Legacy of the Astral Wars*

With all their complexity and paradoxes, the astral wars taught Alex invaluable lessons about conflict, resolution, and the nature of power. They realised that every battle in the astral realm reflected the struggles within the human soul. This journey through the astral battleground was a poignant reminder of *Mahatma Gandhi's teaching: "An eye for an eye only ends up making the whole world blind."*

## *Conclusion*

Alex's experiences in the astral battlegrounds of Eudaimonia offer a vivid exploration of conflict and resolution, extending beyond the physical into the metaphysical realm. These astral wars, with their unique forms of combat and magic, are not just spectacles of power but are deeply symbolic of the inner battles that rage within every individual. Alex's journey reminds us that true strength lies not in the might of arms but in the ability to understand, empathise, and seek balance, echoing the eternal quest for harmony within the human spirit. As a battleground, the astral plane serves as a metaphor for the continuous struggle between opposing forces within and around us, highlighting the importance of inner peace and the impact of our actions on both the seen and unseen worlds.

# CH. 11.

## ALEX AND THE QUEST FOR THE ASTRAL ARTIFACTS

In the enigmatic world of Eudaimonia, the astral plane was a realm of infinite exploration and home to mystical artefacts and keys. These objects held the power to unlock hidden dimensions, offer new modes of travel, or even reveal forbidden areas of the astral realm. Now a seasoned astral traveller, Alex was drawn into an adventure that woven the fabric of magic, mystery, and the quest for these arcane items.

### Part 1: The Call of the Artifacts

Alex's journey began when they learned of the existence of these mystical artefacts from an ancient astral librarian. These objects, scattered across various astral realms, were remnants of a bygone era, each holding unique powers and secrets. *As Carl Jung said, "The meeting of two personalities is like the contact of two chemical substances: if there is any reaction, both are transformed."*

## Part 2: The Map of the Hidden

The first artefact was a map, revealing the locations of the others. This map was not a mere chart but a living, evolving astral entity that responded to the seeker's intentions. It reminded Alex of *T.S. Eliot's profound words: "We shall not cease from exploration, and the end of all our exploring will be to arrive where we started and know the place for the first time."*

## Part 3: The Key of Doors

One of the artefacts, the Key of Doors, allowed access to otherwise sealed realms. This key did not just open physical barriers but also unlocked the potential within the traveller. Holding the key, Alex reflected on a quote by *Paulo Coelho: "When we strive to become better than we are, everything around us becomes better too."*

### Part 4: The Amulet of Perception

Another significant artefact was the Amulet of Perception, which allowed its wearer to see the essence of things beyond illusions and deceptions. Wearing the amulet, Alex understood *Marcel Proust's insight: "The real voyage of discovery consists not in seeking new landscapes, but in having new eyes."*

### Part 5: The Orb of Time

The Orb of Time was a rare artefact that allowed manipulation of astral time, providing glimpses of potential futures and forgotten pasts. Alex experienced the truth of *Albert Einstein's words with the orb: "The distinction between the past, present, and future is only a stubbornly persistent illusion."*

### Part 6: The Conflict over Artifacts

Not all who sought these artefacts had noble intentions. Alex faced adversaries who desired the artefacts for control or domination. In these conflicts, they remembered the wisdom of *Mahatma Gandhi: "Power based on love is a thousand times more effective and permanent than the one derived from fear of punishment."*

## Part 7: The Quest Across Realms

The search for artefacts took Alex across diverse astral realms, each with its challenges and guardians. In these travels, Alex embodied the spirit of adventure and discovery, recalling the words of *Helen Keller: "Life is either a daring adventure or nothing at all."*

## Part 8: The Lesson of the Artifacts

Each artefact, besides its power, held a lesson. The quest was not just a journey across the astral plane but also a journey within. Alex realised the truth of *Rumi's saying: "What you seek is seeking you."*

## Part 9: The Guardian of Artifacts

In the climax of the quest, Alex met the Guardian of Artifacts, an ancient astral being who tested the seekers' intentions. The Guardian reminded Alex of the responsibility that came with power, echoing the words of

*Uncle Ben from Spiderman: "With great power comes great responsibility."*

## Part 10: The Union of Artifacts

The final revelation was that the true power of the artefacts was not in their abilities but in their union. Together, they symbolised the harmony of the astral plane's diverse forces. This union reminded Alex of *Aristotle's concept: "The whole is greater than the sum of its parts."*

## Conclusion

Alex's quest for the mystical artefacts of the astral plane was more than a journey of acquisition; it was a path of self-discovery, understanding, and the responsible use of power. With its unique ability, each artefact taught Alex a fundamental aspect of existence and the interconnectedness of all things. Through this adventure, we, the readers, are invited to reflect on the deeper meanings and responsibilities of pursuing power and knowledge. Alex's journey highlights the importance of intention, wisdom, and collective harmony over individual gain. These artefacts, symbolic of various life aspects, remind us that true mastery lies in understanding and balancing these elements within ourselves and our environment.

## CH. 12.

# ALEX AND THE STAR-CROSSED ECHOES

In the mystical expanses of the astral realm, where souls journeyed beyond the confines of physical existence, a tale of ethereal romance unfolded. This was the story of Alex and Elara, two astral travellers whose paths crossed in the most extraordinary circumstances, bound by a love that transcended realms.

### *Part 1: The First Encounter*

Alex first encountered Elara in a serene astral landscape, where cosmic rivers flowed through starlit skies. Their meeting was unexpected, a rare convergence of astral paths. In Elara's eyes, Alex saw worlds unspoken, and Elara found a warmth that felt like home in Alex's presence. They were reminded of *Rumi's words: "Lovers don't finally meet somewhere. They're in each other all along."*

### Part 2: The Connection of Souls

Their connection was instant, a bond that transcended physicality. Their feelings for each other were amplified in the astral plane, where thoughts and emotions were as tangible as the stars. Each meeting was a confluence of souls, an exhilarating and profound experience. It echoed *Pablo Neruda's verse: "In this part of the story, I am the one who dies, the only one, and I will die of love because I love you."*

### Part 3: The Challenge of Separation

However, their romance faced a poignant challenge. In the physical world, they were separated by insurmountable distances, able to meet only within the astral plane. This separation brought a bittersweet flavour to their love, a longing that intensified with each parting. Their plight resonated with the words of *Nicholas Sparks: "The reason it hurts so much to separate is because our souls are connected."*

## *Part 4: The Language of the Astral*

In their astral meetings, Alex and Elara communicated in a language beyond words, a symphony of emotions and thoughts that wove their spirits closer. Each encounter was a dance of celestial energy, a testament to the power of their bond. They found truth in *Victor Hugo's declaration: "Life's greatest happiness is to be convinced we are loved."*

## *Part 5: The Trials of Love*

Their love was not without trials. As they navigated the challenges of their respective physical lives, their astral meetings became havens of solace and strength. They supported each other's journeys, becoming anchors in the tumultuous sea of life. This trial echoed the words of *Friedrich Nietzsche: "There is always some madness in love. But there is also always some reason in madness."*

## Part 6: The Promise of Eternity

As their connection deepened, Alex and Elara vowed to find each other in the physical world against all odds. This promise was a beacon that guided them, a hope that fueled their determination. It was a romance that defied the constraints of the physical, finding refuge in the boundless expanse of the astral. Their promise was a living embodiment of *Emily Dickinson's words: "Forever is composed of nows."*

## Part 7: The Parallels of Love

Their astral love story was a mirror to the journeys of many souls, a testament to the power of love that bridges worlds. It was a reminder that proper connections are not limited by physical boundaries but are nurtured in the depths of the soul. This sentiment resonated with the philosophy of *Plato: "At the touch of love, everyone becomes a poet."*

## Part 8: The Reunion

As their story progressed, Alex and Elara began to uncover clues in the astral realm that hinted at their physical world locations. Each clue was a step closer to their dream of reunion, a puzzle they solved together with determination and hope. Their quest was akin to a search for a treasure, with love as the ultimate prize.

## Part 9: The Moment of Truth

Finally, after what seemed like an eternity, their paths aligned in the physical world. The moment of their meeting was electric, culminating in all their astral encounters, now manifest in reality. It was a union that blended the ethereal with the earthly, a love that had weathered the trials of separation and distance. In that moment, they understood the depth of *Alfred Lord Tennyson's words: "If I had a flower for every time I thought of you, I could walk through my garden forever."*

## *Part 10: The Everlasting Bond*

Alex and Elara's love story, born in the astral world and fulfilled in the physical world, became a legend in the realms of Eudaimonia. It was a narrative that inspired many, a tale of enduring love that transcended the barriers of worlds. Their journey was a testament to the enduring power of love, echoing the eternal truth in *Lao Tzu's saying: "Being deeply loved by someone gives you strength while loving someone deeply gives you courage."*

## *Conclusion*

Alex and Elara's romance across realms is a narrative that intertwines the mystical with the emotional, encapsulating the longing and fulfilment that comes with true love. Their story transcends the ordinary, offering a glimpse into a love that defies the limitations of physical existence, thriving in the boundless expanses of the astral plane. Through their journey, we are reminded of the profound connections between souls, the power of love to overcome obstacles and the enduring hope that fuels the quest for union. This tale of romance across realms celebrates love's infinite possibilities, echoing across the cosmos as a beacon of hope, inspiration, and the enduring power of the heart's most profound connections.

## CH. 13.

# ALEX AND THE ECHOES OF ETERNITY

In the expansive tapestry of existence, where the threads of life and death interweave, the astral plane stood as a realm beyond the physical, a sanctuary for souls traversing the journey of eternity. This was a world that Alex, an adept astral traveller, came to explore as a mirror of the afterlife, seeking understanding in the mysteries of life, death, and what lay beyond.

### *Part 1: The Gateway to the Beyond*

Alex's journey into this realm of eternal echoes began with a profound realisation, as once stated by *Søren Kierkegaard, "Life can only be understood backwards; but it must be lived forwards."* The astral plane revealed itself as a space for exploration and a reflection of the afterlife, a realm where souls dwelt in post-physical existence.

### *Part 2: The Meeting of Souls*

In this realm, Alex encountered souls from various walks of life, each carrying stories from their earthly existence. These meetings were more than mere encounters; they were exchanges of wisdom, reflections of the lives they once lived. It manifested *Rainer Maria Rilke's thought, "The only journey is the one within."*

### *Part 3: The Realms of Redemption and Reflection*

Alex observed that the astral plane was divided into various realms, each manifesting the soul's journey – realms of redemption, reflection, and growth. Souls here engaged in understanding, learning, and evolving their lives, reminiscent of *Dante Alighieri's journey through the afterlife in "The Divine Comedy."*

### *Part 4: The Mystery of Life and Death*

The astral plane posed profound questions about the nature of existence. Alex pondered these enigmas to understand the fine line between life and death. In this quest, the words of *Khalil Gibran resonated deeply: "For life and death are one, even as the river and the sea are one."*

## Part 5: The Lessons of the Astral

Each soul Alex met imparted different lessons – stories of love, loss, joy, and pain. It was a mosaic of human experience, teaching Alex that every life held profound lessons, however insignificant it might seem. These encounters echoed the wisdom of *Marcus Aurelius: "Accept whatever comes to you woven in the pattern of your destiny, for what could more aptly fit your needs?"*

## Part 6: The Understanding of Karma

The astral plane also revealed the concept of karma – the idea that every action in the physical world resonated into the astral, affecting the soul's journey. This understanding of cause and effect, of moral balancing, was a vivid illustration of *Isaac Newton's third law applied to spiritual existence: "For* every action, there is an equal and opposite reaction."

## Part 7: The Solace of Souls

Many souls found solace in the astral realm, a place for healing and understanding. Alex witnessed these transformations, seeing firsthand the truth in *Elisabeth Kübler-Ross's words: "The most beautiful people we have known are those who have known defeat, known suffering, known struggle, known loss, and have found their way out of the depths."*

## Part 8: The Continuum of Existence

Alex realised that the astral plane was not an end but a continuation, a different phase of existence. It was a realm where the physical and spiritual merged, where the soul's journey was both an ending and a beginning. This realisation was a living testament to *Albert Einstein's belief: "Energy cannot be created or destroyed; it can only be changed from one form to another."*

## Part 9: The Reunion of Loved Ones

One of the most poignant experiences in the astral realm was the reunion of souls. Alex witnessed the joyous meetings of loved ones, a testament to the enduring bonds of affection and love beyond physical existence. It was a profound realisation of love's eternal nature, as beautifully expressed by *Leo Tolstoy: "Only people who are capable of loving strongly can also suffer great sorrow, but this same necessity of loving serves to counteract their grief and heals them."*

## Part 10: The Wisdom of Eternity

Through his explorations, Alex gained wisdom beyond the confines of earthly knowledge. As an afterlife realm, the astral plane was a space of infinite learning, a universe where the mysteries of existence were slowly unravelled. It was a living embodiment of *Socrates' teaching: "To know is to know that you know nothing. That is the meaning of true knowledge."*

## Conclusion

Alex's journey through the astral plane as an afterlife realm was not just an exploration of the mysteries of death but a deeper understanding of life itself. In this ethereal realm, the concepts of time, existence, and consciousness merged into a tapestry of eternal wisdom. Through his encounters and experiences, Alex understood that the astral plane was more than a destination; it reflected the soul's journey – a continuous cycle of learning, evolving, and transcending. This exploration was a profound testament to the interconnectedness of life and death, a reminder that every end is a new beginning and every departure a step towards a new horizon. In the astral plane, the mysteries of life and death unfolded, revealing that existence is an eternal continuum and that in the grand design of the cosmos, every soul is on an infinite journey towards understanding, redemption, and, ultimately, peace.

## CH.14.

# ALEX AND THE NEXUS OF REALMS

Alex found himself at the forefront of a revolution in a future where the boundaries between technology and the human spirit blurred. The advent of a technological interface for astral projection has transformed the landscape of human consciousness, inviting awe-inspiring possibilities and profound ethical dilemmas.

### Part 1: The Dawn of Astral Tech

Alex stood in a world radically altered by technology that enabled controlled astral projection. *Marshall McLuhan famously said, "We shape our tools, and after that, our tools shape us.*" This new technology, a neural interface known as the Nexus, was a testament to this, offering an unprecedented bridge between the physical and astral realms.

## *Part 2: The Euphoria of Discovery*

The initial euphoria surrounding the Nexus was intoxicating. People could now explore astral realms with ease, transcending physical limitations. With his innate ability for astral travel, Alex became a guide in this new era, helping others navigate these uncharted territories. It was a time of boundless exploration, echoing the words of *T.S. Eliot: "Only those who will risk going too far can find out how far one can go."*

## *Part 3: The Ethical Quandaries*

However, the technological marvel soon presented profound ethical questions. The ability to access and manipulate the astral plane raised concerns about privacy, consent, and the sanctity of the soul. As Alex delved more profoundly, he recalled *Aldous Huxley's words: "Technological progress has merely provided us with more efficient means for going backwards."*

## Part 4: The Societal Shift

Society began to shift. Some used the Nexus for spiritual growth and self-discovery, while others sought it for escapism or nefarious purposes. Alex witnessed the widening gap, a society teetering on the edge of utopia and dystopia. It brought to mind Plato's allegory of the cave – were they merely chasing shadows instead of seeking true enlightenment?

## Part 5: The Dilemma of Control

Control became a central theme. Governments and corporations sought to regulate astral travel, leading to debates over freedom and autonomy. Alex found himself amid these conflicts, championing the cause of free will in astral exploration, echoing Benjamin *Franklin's warning: "Those who would give up essential Liberty, to purchase a little temporary Safety, deserve neither Liberty nor Safety."*

## Part 6: The Personal Journey

Amidst the chaos, Alex's journey became more introspective. He pondered the implications of interfacing technology with the human soul. Was this the next step in evolution or a path to losing their essence? In his quest, he remembered *Carl Jung's words: "Who looks outside, dreams; who looks inside, awakes."*

## Part 7: The Anomaly of Consciousness

An unforeseen development occurred when Alex discovered anomalies in the Nexus-induced astral realm – areas where consciousness seemed altered or manipulated. This discovery led him to question the very nature of reality, resonating with *Philip K. Dick's observation: "Reality is that which, when you stop believing in it, doesn't go away."*

## Part 8: The Rebellion of the Spirit

A movement emerged, led by Alex and like-minded individuals, advocating for the responsible use of astral technology. They argued for a balance where technology served as a tool for enhancement rather than domination. Their struggle was a dance on the tightrope of progress, embodying *Einstein's caution: "It has become appallingly obvious that our technology has exceeded our humanity."*

## Part 9: The Resolution

The climax of Alex's journey came with a pivotal discovery – the Nexus had unintentionally tapped into a deeper layer of the astral plane, revealing realms previously unknown. This revelation led to a renaissance in understanding the human spirit, a fusion of technology and consciousness, reminding Alex of *Arthur C. Clarke's adage: "Any sufficiently advanced technology is indistinguishable from magic."*

## Part 10: The New Dawn

In the end, a new equilibrium was reached. Technology and astral projection coexisted, each enhancing the other. The Nexus, now reformed and regulated, became a tool for profound spiritual growth and understanding. Alex looked upon this new world, contemplating the words of *Hermann Hesse: "The bird fights its way out of the egg. The egg is the world. Who would be born must destroy a world."*

## *Conclusion*

Alex's journey through the technological interface with astral projection was a mirror to humanity's eternal quest for understanding. In this futuristic realm, the lines between the spiritual and the technological blurred, creating a tapestry of experiences that challenged and expanded the human psyche. Through trials, revelations, and revolutions, Alex and society learned that technology could open doors to realms beyond imagination when harnessed with wisdom and respect for the human spirit. Yet, they also recognised the need for balance, for in pursuing the unknown, one must never lose sight of the essence that makes us human. In this dance of progress and ethics, humanity found a new path that embraced both the wonders of technology and the depth of the human soul, forging a future where every step was a step towards greater understanding and unity with the cosmos.

## CH. 15.

# ALEX AND THE HEALING BEYOND:
# ASTRAL THERAPISTS IN THE NEW AGE

Alex discovered his calling as an astral explorer and healer in a world where the physical and astral realms intermingled. He belonged to a new breed of therapists who transcended traditional boundaries of medicine and psychology. He used astral travel to heal the deepest wounds of the mind and, miraculously, the body.

## Part 1: The Emergence of Astral Therapy

Alex's journey into astral healing began with a profound realisation. *Hippocrates once said, "Healing is a matter of time, but it is sometimes also a matter of opportunity."* Astral therapy provided an opportunity to access and heal parts of the psyche unreachable by conventional methods.

## Part 2: The Healing Process

Astral therapy sessions were unlike any other. Clients, guided by Alex, journeyed into their astral selves, confronting traumas and fears in a realm where physical limitations did not exist. The process was akin to dream therapy but on a far deeper level. Alex often mused *Carl Jung's words, "Your visions will become clear only when you can look into your heart. Who looks outside, dreams; who looks inside, awakes."*

## Part 3: Healing the Mind

The most striking success was psychological. Individuals who struggled with deep-seated emotional scars found solace and resolution in the astral realm. Alex helped them confront and accept their shadows, leading to profound healing and transformation.

## Part 4: The Mystery of Physical Healing

Surprisingly, astral therapy had physical effects. Clients reported alleviating chronic pain and, in some cases, improving physiological conditions. Though not fully understood, it seemed the mind's journey in the astral plane could trigger natural physical healing, echoing the words of *Paracelsus: "The spirit is the master; imagination the tool, and the body the plastic material."*

### Part 5: The Ethical Implications

With these successes came ethical considerations. The power of astral therapy was immense, and the potential for misuse was a concern. Alex often grappled with these issues, striving to maintain integrity and empathy, believing, as *Rumi said, "The wound is the place where the Light enters you."*

### Part 6: Training and Responsibility

Alex embarked on training other therapists in the art of astral healing. It was a journey of skill, personal growth, and responsibility. He emphasised therapists' need first to explore their astral landscapes, as true healing begins within.

## Part 7: The Challenges of Acceptance

Despite its successes, astral therapy faced scepticism. The medical and scientific communities struggled with its intangible nature. Alex worked tirelessly to bridge this gap, advocating for a holistic health view encompassing body, mind, and spirit.

## Part 8: The Collective Healing

Alex's vision extended beyond individual therapy. He saw the potential for astral healing to address collective traumas and societal wounds. In a world of conflict and pain, astral therapy offered a path to a deeper, more compassionate understanding of humanity.

## Part 9: The Personal Journey of a Healer

Alex's journey was transformative. Each session, each dive into another's psyche, changed him, deepening his empathy and understanding of the human condition. He lived the truth of *Nietzsche's words: "He who has a why to live can bear almost any how."*

### Part 10: The Future of Healing

As Alex looked towards the future, he saw a world where astral therapy was integral to healing. He envisioned a society where the exploration of the astral realm was not just for personal enlightenment but for the betterment of all.

## *Conclusion*

Alex found his true purpose in the realm of astral healers and therapists. By blending the ancient wisdom of the spirit with the modern understanding of the psyche, he and his fellow healers opened a new frontier in medicine and therapy. They showed that the healing journey was not just a path walked in the physical world but also a voyage into the depths of the soul. In doing so, they offered hope, healing, and a new way to understand the intricate tapestry of the human experience, rooted in the profound belief that within the vast and mysterious realms of the astral lay the keys to our most profound healing and understanding.

## CH. 16.

# Epilogue:

# Beyond the Veil - A Philosophical Closure to Astral Odysseys

As the chronicles of Alex and the astral realms draw to a serene close, we find ourselves standing at the threshold of comprehension, gazing into the infinite tapestry of existence. This epilogue is not merely a conclusion but a contemplative pause, a moment to reflect on the profound journey through the astral plane and the philosophical insights it has unveiled.

### *Part 1: The Integration of Experiences*

Alex's journey across the astral realms has been a kaleidoscope of experiences, each coloured with the hues of enlightenment and self-discovery. Like the mythical Phoenix rising from its ashes, Alex transforms from his astral travels, carrying the wisdom of a thousand worlds with him. His journey epitomises the words of *Marcel Proust, "The real voyage of discovery consists not in seeking new landscapes, but in having new eyes."*

## Part 2: The Unity of Existence

The interconnectedness of the astral realms has revealed a fundamental truth - the unity of all existence. In this unity, the barriers between self and other, the physical and the metaphysical, dissolve, echoing the words of the philosopher *Alan Watts, "You are not a drop in the ocean. You are the entire ocean in a drop."*

## Part 3: The Transcendence of Time and Space

In his travels, Alex has transcended the conventional bounds of time and space, experiencing the fluidity of existence. This transcendence is a testament to the boundless potential of consciousness and a reflection of the words of *William Blake, "To see a World in a Grain of Sand and a Heaven in a Wild Flower, Hold Infinity in the palm of your hand And Eternity in an hour."*

## Part 4: The Ethical Awakening

The ethical dilemmas and moral choices Alex encountered in the astral realms have culminated in an ethical awakening, highlighting the interconnectedness of actions and consequences. This echoes Immanuel Kant's imperative to act in ways that respect the dignity of all beings, a reminder of the profound impact of our choices.

## Part 5: The Personal and Collective Journey

Alex's astral odyssey, while deeply personal, mirrors the collective journey of humanity. His experiences are a microcosm of the human quest for meaning and understanding, reflecting the existential musings of philosophers through the ages.

## Part 6: The Harmonization of Science and Spirituality

Alex's adventures in the astral plane represent the harmonisation of science and spirituality, a fusion that expands our understanding of the universe. This convergence is a reminder of the words of *Albert Einstein, "Science without religion is lame; religion without science is blind."*

### Part 7: The Continuity of the Quest

As we reach the end of this narrative, it becomes clear that the quest for knowledge and self-discovery is a continuous journey. Each answer unravels new questions, and each discovery opens new frontiers, as beautifully articulated by *Rainer Maria Rilke, "Be patient toward all that is unsolved in your heart and try to love the questions themselves."*

## *Conclusion: The Infinite Echo*

The stories of Alex and the astral realms are more than just tales of mystical adventures; they explore the depths of human consciousness and the mysteries of existence. As this saga concludes, it leaves behind an echo, a resonant reminder of the unending journey of the soul through the boundless realms of the astral and beyond.

In the words of *Lao Tzu, "The journey of a thousand miles begins with a single step."*

Alex's astral odyssey may have reached its narrative end, but the philosophical journey continues, ever-expanding. The astral plane, with its myriad realms and endless possibilities, remains a cosmic canvas, inviting each one of us to paint our journey of discovery and enlightenment.

And so, as we close this chapter, we understand that it is not an end but a new beginning, a perpetual voyage into the vast, uncharted territories of the astral and the self, where every end is a new beginning and every conclusion, a new genesis.

# About the Author

https://www.amazon.com/stores/author/B0987KMMTP/about

## Mr. SWAMINATHAN MURALI

*A doyen with a rich experience of 33 years in the Oil Field. Being a Science talent scholar, he has done his M.Sc. (Hons) in Chemistry and M.Sc. (Hons) in Biological Sciences from the prestigious Birla Institute of Technology & Science, BITS PILANI, an*

*MBA with specialisation in Operations Research, Oracle Certified Data Base Manager, Black Belt in Six Sigma and a PMP certified Professional of PMPs-USA.*

*On joining the prestigious Maharatna E & P company, he rose to the Head of Material Management level with a score of officers and staff under his guidance and mentorship until his superannuation.*

**Contact Author - smuralis2000@gmail.com**

# A Humble Request For Your Valuable Review

*Could you please leave a review on the book? One last time! I'd love it if you could leave a review about the book. Reviews may not matter to big-name authors, but they're a tremendous help for authors like me, who don't have much following. They help me grow my readership by encouraging folks to take a chance on my books. To put it straight– reviews are the lifeblood of any author. Please leave your review by clicking the below link; it will directly lead you to the book review page.*

### "Realms of the Astral Plane"
### https://www.amazon.com/dp/B0C74B47YX

*It will take less than a minute of yours, but it will tremendously help me reach out to more people, so please leave your review. Thank you for supporting my work, and I'd love to see your book review.*

# RHYTHM OF LIFE:

**E-book link:** https://www.amazon.com/dp/B0C74B47YX

**Paperback link:**

https://www.amazon.com/dp/B0C87VXZH6

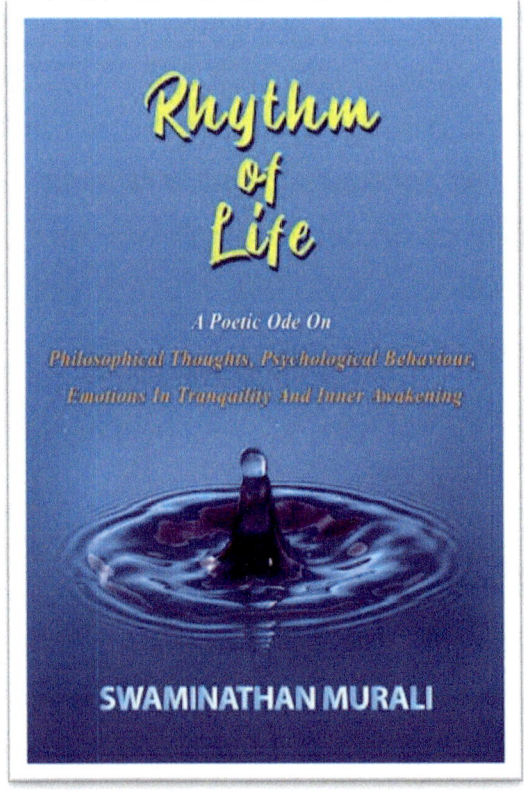

"Rhythm of Life" is a captivating collection of poetic verses that serve as an eloquent ode to philosophical thoughts, psychological behaviour, emotions in tranquillity, and inner awakening. This book attempts to take the readers on a mesmerising journey through the depths of the human experience, weaving together profound insights and heartfelt emotions with the grace and beauty of poetry.

Through the power of language and metaphor, "Rhythm of Life" delves into the core of existence, exploring the intricate tapestryof life's philosophical underpinnings. The author skillfully navigates through complex ideas, inviting readers to ponder the nature of reality, the purpose of our existence, and the interconnectedness of all things. Each line draws the reader deeper into the intricate web of existence, where profound questions and timeless wisdom intertwine.

In addition to its philosophical depth, "Rhythm of Life" delves intopsychological behaviour, offering keen observations on the human mind and its intricate workings. The poems vividly portray the human psyche through vivid imagery and evocative language, exploring themes of love, loss, resilience, and growth.The author's words become a mirror that reflects our thoughts, fears, desires, and joys, inviting us to embark on a journey of self-discovery and introspection.

One of the book's remarkable strengths is its ability to evoke emotions in tranquillity. The author's words carry a certain serenity, gently guiding readers to find solace and peace amidstthe chaos of life. Each poem acts as a gentle embrace, comforting weary souls and reminding us of the inherent beauty and harmony within ourselves and the world around us. The author's words carry a certain serenity, gently guiding readers tofind solace and peace amidst the chaos of life.

Finally, "Rhythm of Life" catalyses inner awakening. It encourages readers to embark on a personal journey of self-discovery, urging them to explore the depths of their souls and embrace their true essence. The poems inspire introspection, encouraging readers to question their beliefs, challenge societalnorms, and uncover their authentic selves. Through its profound wisdom and gentle guidance, the book becomes a companion on the path to self-realisation and inner transformation.

"Rhythm of Life" is a testament to the power of poetry to illuminate the human experience. It is a *lyrical masterpiece that touches the heart, stimulates the mind, and stirs the soul. With its insightful verses and enchanting imagery, this book invites readers to embark on a profound and introspective journey, awakening a deeper understanding of themselves and the world they inhabit.*

*In the depths of our being resides a flickering flame that yearns to illuminate our lives with its gentle glow. It is the flame of happiness, a beacon of light that can transform our existence and awaken us to the true essence of our being.*

*"The Art of Waking Up to Happiness" invites you to embark on a profound journey that transcends the boundaries of time and space, reaching deep into the core of your being. This book is not a mere collection of words on pages; it is a heartfelt invitation to explore the boundless potential within you.*

*Within these pages, you will encounter a mosaic of philosophical thoughts, psychological insights, emotional revelations, and practical strategies - carefully woven together to guide you on a transformative path. As you immerse yourself in this exploration, you will discover that happiness is not a distant destination but a state of being that can be awakened and nurtured within the fabric of your everyday life.*

*"The Art of Waking Up to Happiness" is an invitation to let go of the illusions that bind you, to release the burdens of the past, and to embrace the present moment with open arms. It delves into the depths of our human experience, exploring the intricate tapestry of our thoughts, emotions, and behaviours. It offers insights to guide you towards a more joyful and fulfilling existence.*

*As you embark on this journey, remember that change does not happen overnight. It requires patience, perseverance, and a willingness to confront the shadows that lie within. The road may be winding, and you may stumble upon obstacles and challenges, but know that within you resides a wellspring of resilience and strength.*

*Through each passing day, you will uncover daily snippets of wisdom, guiding you towards a deeper understanding of yourself and the world around you. This is an opportunity to cultivate a new way of being that embraces the beauty of life, finds meaning in the smallest moments, and radiates the vibrant hues of happiness.*

*Embrace this journey with an open heart and an open mind. Allow the words to resonate within you, gently nudging you towards a more expansive and authentic existence. The time has come to awaken to the art of waking up to happiness - to embark on a transformational voyage towards a life filled with joy, purpose, and a persistent connection to your inner light.*

# BOOKS FROM THE AUTHOR

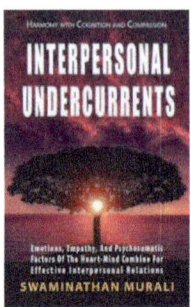

### INTERPERSONAL UNDERCURRENTS

Emotions, Empathy, And Psychosomatic Factors of the Heart-Mind Combine for Effective Interpersonal Relations
http://tinyurl.com/3k4cndtj

### HONING TEAM-BUILDING SKILLS FROM NATURE

Art of building Strong Cohesive, Collaborative Teams; Understanding importance of Emotional Intelligence in Leadership
http://tinyurl.com/z4a6f8hy

### THE COGNITIVE EMOTIONAL INTELLIGENCE

Exploring impacts of Emotional Intelligence in our lives, Evaluation of EI, Improving Self-awareness with Compassion ... Empathy. (EMOTIONS IN TRANQUILITY Book 1)
http://tinyurl.com/mpcnmte4

### THE ART OF WAKING UP TO HAPPINESS

Awakening Happiness And Unveiling The Path To Blissful Success, Embracing Joy, And Navigating Life's Purposeful Journey

http://tinyurl.com/mpefa4w2

# MORE BOOKS FROM THE AUTHOR

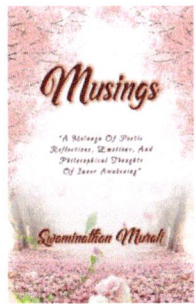

**MUSINGS**
A Melange Of Poetic Reflections,
Emotions,
And Philosophical Thoughts Of Inner
Awakening
http://tinyurl.com/2p8nnvvx

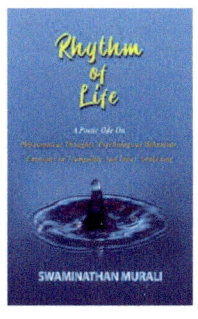

**RHYTHM OF LIFE**
A Poetic Ode on Philosophical Thoughts,
Psychological Behaviour, Emotions In
Tranquility And Inner Awakening
http://tinyurl.com/hej77hbw

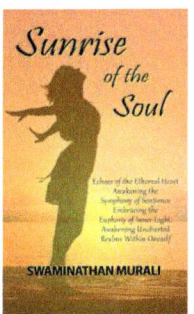

**SUNRISE OF THE SOUL:**

Echoes of the Etherial Heart, Awakening
the Symphony of Sentience, Embracing
the Euphony of Inner Light, Awakening
Uncharted Realms
https://tinyurl.com/529hzakb

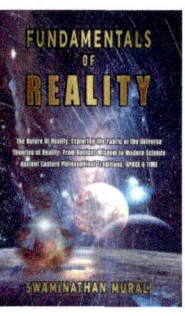

**FUNDAMENTALS OF REALITY:**

Bridging Science and Philosophy:
Delving into Quantum Realms,
Cosmic Mysteries, and the Time-
Space Continuum for Transformative
https://tinyurl.com/mry7fxa4

# Acknowledgement

This entire compilation would not have taken this shape without the soul-inspiring encouragement from Mr Ranjit Jose, who was instrumental in the beautiful cover and interior design and a mentor in the finer aspects of the intricacies of the layout and design.

I am grateful to Bing AI for ably assisting with the internal figures/images.

I will fail in my duty if I do not acknowledge the understanding and cooperation of my wife, Latha, for her encouragement.

Last but not least, I thank my son and daughter for their support and my two lovely grandchildren, who ensured my attention in scribbling this book.

# COPYRIGHT

## Copyright©2024SwaminathanMurali

*All rights reserved. No part of this publication may be reproduced or transmitted in any form or by any means, mechanical or electronic, including photocopying or recording, by any information storage and retrieval system, or by email or any other means whatsoever without permission in writing from the author. No part of this book may be reproduced in any form without permission in writing from the author.*

For any queries, please feel free to contact me at

## smuralis2000@gmail.com

Printed in Dunstable, United Kingdom